ALL TO PLAY FOR

EVE AINSWORTH

ILLUSTRATED BY
KIRSTI BEAUTYMAN

Barrington Stoke

First published in 2022 in Great Britain by
Barrington Stoke Ltd
18 Walker Street, Edinburgh, EH3 7LP

www.barringtonstoke.co.uk

A CIP catalogue record for this book is available from the British Library upon request

ISBN: 978-1-80090-092-9

Printed by Hussar Books, Poland

To the children of Milton Mount Primary School. Always strive to be the best you can be.

Chapter 1

Lewis was in his happy place.

It was just a strip of grass at the back of the estate where he lived. At one end stood the bins, where residents stacked up their rubbish and recycling. At the other end was the small, crowded car park.

But here, in the shadow of the tower blocks, Lewis could slam his ball against the grey wall that lay between the Seven Hills estate and the main road. And no one would bother him.

It was the start of the summer holidays and Lewis was glad that he had more time to spend outside.

Lewis didn't care that the road was just behind him. He blocked out the noise of the traffic and the sounds of music and chatter from the flats. All his focus was on controlling the ball. He loved the sound it made.

Thud, thud, thud.

Lewis carefully controlled every rebound with his right foot and then kicked it back to the wall with his left. He was trying to hit the same spot every time – a grey brick right in front of him. He needed to be dead accurate. He could feel his frustration grow every time he missed it even by a few centimetres. He would never get better if he kept doing that.

The ball wasn't a good one. His mum wouldn't buy him one, so Jermaine, his best mate, had given Lewis one of his old ones. It used to be bright yellow, but the colour had faded a bit. There were patches where it was going bald, and it was heavy and flat.

Lewis didn't mind. Any ball was better than none. He kept it hidden in a tiny gap behind the bin store and every evening before his tea he came outside to practise.

Just across from the estate was the park and playing fields where most of the older boys played. Lewis watched them sometimes. They were tall and clumsy and shouted at each other a lot. It looked to Lewis as if they spent more time taking each other out than actually playing a decent game.

He had gone across once to ask if he could play, but that had been a mistake. They had laughed at his old trainers and said he was "skinny" and "weak". Lewis didn't bother asking again.

Anyway, he liked it here behind the tower blocks because it was quiet. No one could disturb him or wind him up. No one took any notice of him.

He liked it here because he could pretend to be somebody else. As he slammed the ball once more against the wall, hitting the grey brick perfectly, he raised his arms in the air, a tiny smile stretching across his face.

Just for a moment he could pretend he was like his hero, Sancho. At Wembley. Scoring the winning goal for England.

A proper footballer.

That was the best dream of all.

"Hey, Lewis!"

He looked up. Jermaine and Harry were standing by the car park, waving him over. Jermaine's dad was in the car waiting for them. They were dressed in bright blue football kits. Lewis looked down at their feet and then at his. They both had the newest and best boots on, not like his scruffy trainers. He knew those boots were really expensive. And that made him feel even more left out.

Lewis picked up his ball and strolled over. He felt shy, which was silly really. Jermaine had been his best friend since Nursery. Even so, he didn't like people seeing him practising.

"Are you going to training?" Lewis asked.

Jermaine went to a football training school called Ace Academy on the other side of town. It was meant to be a really good one. Jermaine had been nagging Lewis to go for ages, but Lewis knew his mum would never agree. Now the training school was running a club over the summer holidays and Jermaine was going to it.

Jermaine nodded. "Dad's taking us now." He looked slowly over at Lewis. "It would be great if you could come one time, Lew? We could take you too."

"Yeah, you should come," Harry said. "You'd be so good."

Lewis smiled. "Nah – it's OK. I'm not bothered about training. I'm not into it that badly."

It was so easy to lie. Lewis knew Jermaine could see right through it, but his friend didn't say anything. Instead, he just nodded slowly.

"Well – the offer is there, yeah?" Jermaine said.

"Thanks."

Lewis watched as the boys piled into the car. Jermaine's dad gave him a friendly wave. Lewis felt small and sad as he watched them pull away. A part of him longed to run after them, to call them back. To tell them that he had been wrong. He did want to go. He wanted to go more than anything. But Lewis had found out how much the football school cost ages ago and it was really expensive.

Lewis walked back over to the bin store and carefully pushed his ball back into its hiding hole.

It didn't matter anyway. Even if she could afford it, Mum would never let him play football.

Not after what happened to his dad.

Chapter 2

Lewis lived on the eighth floor. He always took the stairs because it was good exercise and also because the lifts were smelly and sometimes broke down. Lewis liked to run up the stairs to really work his leg muscles. By the time he reached his floor, he was panting hard.

Outside his door, he could smell his mum's cooking. His stomach immediately began to growl. He opened the door and ran in, hoping that it was his favourite – spaghetti and meatballs.

Mum was in the kitchen, stirring the pan. At her feet was their huge, scruffy dog, Trevor. Trev trotted over to Lewis as soon as he saw him. Trev's fur was rough and shaggy, and he had big wise eyes. Mum had rescued him years ago from owners who weren't treating him properly. Trev was really old now and sometimes his legs didn't work very well. His bark was a bit croaky, but Lewis loved him to bits. He was the best dog in the world.

"How was the park?" Mum asked.

"OK."

"What did you do?"

"Nothing really, just hung about."

"Was that all you did?" she asked.

"Yeah."

Lewis didn't like lying to his mum, but he knew that she wouldn't be happy about him practising football. She would think he was getting back into it again. He used to play outside with Jermaine and some other kids from the estate, but he'd stopped when he'd seen how it was upsetting his mum.

He peered into the pan and saw his mum was cooking his favourite dinner. Right away he felt better.

"You're hungry?" she asked, ruffling his hair.

"Yeah. Starving," he answered.

It was just the three of them now. Lewis, his mum and Trevor. His dad had died when Lewis was a baby, so he didn't remember him. In the living room there was a photo of his dad. He was with Mum and Lewis. Lewis was only a few months old then, sitting on his lap. Mum had her arms wrapped around him. They had been a happy family. You could tell.

There was another photo. Lewis had seen it, but his mum kept it hidden in the cupboard under the TV. She took it out sometimes when she thought Lewis was in his room. She would often be crying. In this photo, Lewis's dad was playing football. It was an action shot – he was running down the wing about to score. He looked strong and athletic.

Lewis's mum said his dad had been the best footballer ever.

She also said it was football that killed him. His heart had been weak and during one awful game it had stopped working altogether. There had been nothing anyone could do.

A year ago, Lewis had asked his mum if he could go to football training with Jermaine and Harry. It was when they had first started going to Ace Academy and he'd wanted to go too.

His mum had just frowned. At first she said it would be too expensive. But then she said that she didn't want him taking up his "time and energy" with a sport that had already messed up their lives. She had looked across at the family photo of when Lewis was a baby. There were tears welling in her eyes.

"Football only brings us heartache, Lewis," she said softly. "I'd rather you did anything else. Just not that."

He didn't say any more after that. He didn't want to upset her.

That's why Lewis could never tell his mum the truth now. He could never talk about his hopes and dreams. Because he didn't want to break her heart all over again.

Chapter 3

Lewis didn't really know much about his dad. Every time his mum talked about him, she either got very upset or very angry. So it was easier not to ask. He wished he knew more though. He didn't want his dad to feel like a stranger.

The few things that Lewis knew about him were that:

a. His name was Jeremy, he was tall – 6 foot 1 inches – and he died when he was 26, only 14 years older than Lewis was now.

Lewis thought he looked a little like him, except his own skin was lighter. They had the same shaped eyes and nose, and Lewis was already one of the tallest in his class.

b. Jeremy had been born on an island called Mauritius. He moved to England when he was the same age as Lewis was now – 12. After he died, Jeremy's mum and aunties moved back to Mauritius. They wrote letters and called, but Lewis didn't really know them very well. He wished he could visit them. He hoped to when he was older.

c. Jeremy worked as a gardener. Mum told Lewis that he knew loads about plants and flowers. He could make anything grow, but he was also a part-time footballer. He played for the local football team – Deansgate Town. Mum said he was good enough to play for a bigger team, but he hurt his knee when he was younger. She said he had been for trials with other clubs and spent a year at the Crystal Palace Academy.

Mum told him that Jeremy's smile lit up the room and that he was the kindest, gentlest man she'd ever known. She missed him every day.

Lewis sometimes thought about what it would be like if his dad was still around. He could picture him, like a shadow next to him, helping him along. He felt his dad most when he had the football at his feet. He could almost hear his dad's voice praising him as he struck the ball, telling him he was doing well. He liked to think that his dad was proud of him.

He only wished his mum felt the same.

Chapter 4

The next day, Lewis was back in his same safe hidden spot near the bins. The sun was warm on his back as he worked on his keepie-uppies. There had been no point knocking for Jermaine, as he would be back at the holiday football school today. It didn't matter anyway. Lewis was happy to focus on his skills. On his own, he could concentrate much better.

"Hey, mate. Looking sharp."

Lewis looked up quickly. Who had said that? The ball knocked clumsily against his knee and rolled towards the stranger standing just behind him. Actually, he wasn't really a stranger. Lewis knew him from around the estate. He was tall and strong, dressed in an expensive-looking tracksuit. His dark hair was twisted into tight cornrows. He had a large bag slung over his shoulder.

Lewis blinked back at him, suddenly feeling shy. He knew he must look scruffy with his old clothes and scrappy trainers. He swiped at his sweaty face.

"I'm Ash," the man said. "I live in your block. Your mum is Alison, right?"

Lewis nodded. "Yeah. I'm Lewis."

"I couldn't help noticing how good you are with the ball," said Ash. "Do you do any training anywhere?"

"No." Lewis shrugged. "I just practise out here."

"You're really good. You have great control. I was counting – you kept that ball up for ages." Ash grinned. "And I saw the trick, the 'around the world'. Took me years to master that."

Lewis couldn't help smiling. Around the world is a skill where you bring the ball behind your leg and back round to the front in one move. It had taken him quite a while to get it right.

"How's your other skills? Shooting? Dribbling?" Ash asked.

"I like dribbling best," Lewis said. "I use skills I see on the internet. Flip-flaps, rabonas ..."

These were all tricks used to fool a defender when you were running with the ball. Lewis liked to practise them over and over, pretending that he was taking part in a real match.

"Here, show me your control," Ash said, throwing his bag on the ground and taking the ball. He drove the ball towards Lewis, and Lewis quickly met it using his left foot, bringing the ball down neatly and firmly in front of him. He then played it back to Ash's feet.

"Control it with your chest now," Ash said as he lofted the ball towards him. Lewis did that, rushing to meet the ball with his chest pushed out. He controlled the ball easily, bringing it back down to his feet. Ash nodded in approval.

"Do you play for a team?" Ash asked.

"No."

"You never have?"

Lewis shrugged again. "My mum won't let me."

Ash frowned. "Why not?"

Lewis felt his face grow hot. He didn't want to explain about his dad. He didn't know if this guy would understand. Jermaine and Harry didn't. They always said his mum was just "acting crazy". He decided to stick with the simple excuse instead. It was easier and also true.

"She can't afford it. The signing-on fees, the kit, the boots. Getting me to games ..." Lewis's voice drifted. "It's too expensive I guess."

Ash nodded again and said, "Yeah, it can be."

Lewis scuffed at the ball. He felt both frustrated and embarrassed. And he hated talking about this sort of stuff. He hated people feeling sorry for him. He just wished things were different.

Ash was reaching down towards his bag and digging through it. Lewis watched as he pulled out a leaflet. He stood up again and held it towards Lewis. Lewis could see the words "ACE ACADEMY" written across the front. It was the same football school that Jermaine and Harry went to. Lewis realised that Ash must be one of their coaches.

"This is the football academy I help to manage," he said. "We're running sessions throughout the summer. I'd like you to come along, Lewis. I think with some training you could be really good."

"But we can't afford—"

Ash held out his hand. "You can have some free sessions. On me. Talk to your mum about it. It's at Deansgate's ground."

Deansgate – where his dad used to play.

"I'd love you to come," Ash said. "I really think I could help you."

Chapter 5

Lewis slipped into the stairwell with the leaflet still in his hand. His heart was beating fast. He kept re-reading the words that were printed on it:

> *Ace Academy – improve your football skills with the best coaching around!*
>
> *Be the best. Believe in yourself. Achieve.*

He blinked at the words. Believe in yourself. Could he? Could he really be the best? In the school playground, Harry and Jermaine were always complaining that he was faster than them and more skilful – but that was just school. And they were his mates and probably just being nice.

He thought of his mum. She was out working at the moment – busy cleaning huge offices. She would come home tired with a sore head and back. If he showed her this leaflet, if he told her about this, he knew what she'd say. She had said it to him before.

"You don't want to do this, Lewis. Football is a horrible sport. It's expensive and competitive. Look what happened to your father. Focus on school. Focus on anything but this."

She wouldn't want to talk about it. She would just shut him down or get upset.

Lewis screwed the leaflet up into a tight ball and stuffed it into his pocket. There was no point talking to her about it. It would just lead to more bad feelings.

And Lewis knew he couldn't face that.

*

A little later, Lewis took Trevor for a short walk around the flats. He couldn't go far because of Trevor's wobbly legs, but the dog liked to have a sniff of the grass and nose about. Lewis liked to see him happy.

As they passed the grassy patch outside the main doors, Lewis saw Harry and Jermaine sitting on the low wall that ran alongside the path. They obviously had just come back from training as they were still in their football gear and looked sweaty. Jermaine waved him over.

"Trevor!" he said happily, diving towards the dog and ruffling his fur. "Man, you are the best dog ever, I swear."

"How was training?" Lewis asked.

Harry grinned. "It was so good. They're putting on a tournament for us soon against the local academies. Mate, you should be there."

Jermaine nodded. "Seriously, you would love it."

"I was chatting to this guy today," Lewis said. "He saw me practising. He gave me a leaflet for your football school. His name was Ash."

"You're kidding me," laughed Jermaine. "He's the guy that runs the place. He's really cool."

"He said I can have some free sessions," Lewis said.

Jermaine's eyes looked like they would pop out of his head. "For real? You must have impressed him. He can be really fussy. He was a great player too."

“He used to play for the Arsenal youth team, but he got injured,” Harry added.

“Ash?” Lewis said. “Wow.”

“That’s right.” Jermaine still looked stunned. “Seriously, mate. You need to go for this. If Ash spotted you, it’s a really good sign. He must think you’re good.”

Beside him, Trevor pulled at the lead, getting bored with the chatter. Lewis bent down and gently rubbed his head to soothe him. Maybe his legs were hurting.

"You are going, right?" Harry asked. "Your mum will understand. It's free, right? It's not like she has to pay."

"It's not just that," Lewis said. "It's not only about the money. It's my dad and stuff." He sighed. "And even if she was OK, I need boots and that. It all adds up ..."

"I have some old ones," Jermaine told him. "We're about the same size. Come over later."

"Thanks, mate," Lewis said.

Jermaine patted Trev's head again and looked back at Lewis. "You need to talk to your mum. You need to explain how important it is to you. You can't throw this sort of opportunity away. It doesn't happen all the time."

Trevor gave a low bark beside him as if he was saying that he agreed.

"Maybe ..." Lewis shook his head, still unsure.

It had been a few months since he last asked his mum about playing football, so she might have changed her mind by now. And everyone knew that what had happened to his dad was a freak event. Even his nan had said so in her letters to Lewis. No one had known anything about his dad's weak heart. He must've been born with it. Why couldn't his mum see that too?

She couldn't keep blaming football for what happened to his dad.

Chapter 6

Lewis knew he had to pick the right time to talk to his mum, but he wasn't sure when that would be. It was already evening, almost bedtime, and he hadn't said anything yet.

Instead, he stared at the photo of his dad that he had taken out of the cupboard. Trevor was beside Lewis on the sofa, a lovely warm bundle of fluff, snoring gently and now and then making odd snuffling noises. His legs kicked out as he dreamed.

He could hear his mum in the bathroom, taking a shower after work. She wasn't singing today. When she sang in the shower, Lewis knew she'd had a good day. When she was quiet, he knew she was tired or worried about something. Tonight wasn't the best time to talk to her about Ash and his offer.

The photo of his dad seemed to shine back at Lewis as he stared at it. He looked so handsome and strong. His face was determined and his expression focused as he ran with the ball. Lewis wished, not for the first time, that the picture could come alive and he could see his dad play in front of him.

"What would my dad say?" Lewis asked the sleeping Trevor. "Would he let me go, even after what happened to him? Would he want me to do it?"

Trevor made a grunting noise. He lifted his head and looked at Lewis with sad, sleepy eyes.

Lewis carefully took the photo and walked into his bedroom. He slipped the picture under his pillow, where it could be safe. Where it would be close to him.

He felt the heavy shift on his bed as Trevor pulled himself up beside Lewis, grunting a bit, like he was complaining about being moved. Curling himself around Trevor's warm body, Lewis's hand slipped under the pillow and touched the photo of his dad. As he closed his eyes, he imagined he was on the pitch, running, dribbling, crossing the ball.

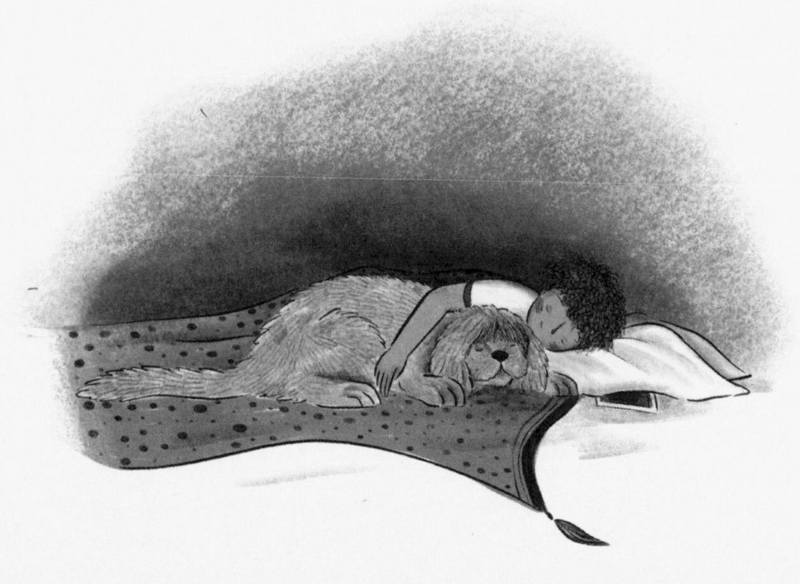

Across the pitch his dad stood, proud and smiling and cheering him on.

Both Trevor and Lewis dreamed they were in their happy place.

Chapter 7

Lewis woke up late the next morning. He went into the kitchen for breakfast. His mum had already put the bread in the toaster and poured him a glass of fresh orange juice. Trevor moved round at her feet in circles, looking for scraps. He might be old, but he was always begging for food like a puppy.

"Morning, sleepy-head." His mum bent down and planted a kiss on Lewis's head. He could smell her sweet flowery perfume and her lemon shower cream. She always smelled of summer to him. "You must've been tired out yesterday, you fell asleep so early."

Lewis thought of all the football practice he had done and nodded. He had slept really well, but his thoughts this morning were full of Ash and what he'd said.

His mum was buttering the toast, humming along with the music playing on the radio. As she passed him the plate, her dark eyes fixed on him carefully.

"I picked your dirty washing up off the floor. You just left it there for me to find."

Lewis dipped his head. "Sorry, Mum, I was so tired."

"Well – you know better. Putting it in the washing bin is no effort really, is it?" She waited a moment. He noticed she was chewing on her bottom lip. "I checked the pockets before

I put your shorts in the washing machine. I found this."

She reached across the worktop and picked up a crumpled leaflet. Lewis felt his stomach twist. The bit of toast in his mouth was suddenly dry and tasteless. He couldn't swallow it.

"Lewis," his mum said, "who gave you this?"

"His name is Ash. He lives on our block."

"Ash." She seemed to be thinking. "What – Ashley Thomas? The tall kid? The ex-footballer? Bernice's lad?"

Lewis shrugged. He had no clue who Ash's mum was, but he knew that his own mum knew practically everyone on the estate. It would make sense that she knew Ash too.

"Why were you talking to him?" she asked.

"He saw me." Lewis looked down at the table. "I was practising."

His mum frowned. "Practising? But I thought you weren't interested in playing football any more. I thought we agreed?"

You agreed, Lewis wanted to say, but he didn't want to upset his mum. He knew it wasn't her fault really.

"I'm sorry," he muttered instead.

"You don't even have a ball," she said, still sounding puzzled.

"Jermaine gave me an old one of his," Lewis replied, pushing his toast to one side. He wasn't hungry now. "I don't do much, Mum. Just a few tricks and skills. I ... I like it."

"And this Ash saw you?"

"Yeah. He said I was good. He wants me to come along for a few sessions. He said he could help me."

His mum shook her head slowly. "Even if I wanted you to, you know I can't, Lewis. These things cost a fortune. I'm struggling to make ends meet as it is."

Lewis sat up, his heart hammering. "But that's the thing – Ash said I can have some free sessions. It won't cost us anything."

He blurted out the words, thinking his mum might be pleased. He thought it might take away one of her worries, but he saw right away that he had made a mistake. She scowled, then tossed the crumpled leaflet across the table.

"You're not going, Lewis."

Lewis felt like his heart was going to burst from his chest. "I don't understand, Mum. It's just a few sessions, that's all. It's free. I just want to try it. Dad would—"

"Don't bring your dad into this," she snapped. "You don't know."

"But—"

She held out her hand. "You're not going and I'm taking you over to Ashley's flat now to explain why." Her eyes flashed with anger

as she reached for her handbag and front-door key. "We might be poor, Lewis, and we might struggle for money, but we don't need to take anyone's charity – do you hear me? Now come with me. We need to thank Ashley kindly for his time, but we also need to say no thank you."

Chapter 8

Ash lived in the same block as Lewis but on the ground floor. As they approached his door, Lewis saw that there was a pair of muddy football boots on the mat outside. His insides felt like jelly. He wished that his mum hadn't insisted on coming to Ash's place like this – but he knew that when his mum got an idea in her head there was no stopping her.

She rapped on the door and stepped back, waiting, her hands on her hips. When Ash opened the door, he saw Lewis's mum first and then Lewis. He smiled.

“Hello, Ashley,” Lewis’s mum said politely. “Do you remember me?”

“Of course I do, Mrs Marie. You know my mum, Bernice.”

She nodded. “I do and I’ve known you since you were a small boy.”

Lewis noticed that there was a trace of a smile on her lips. His mum didn’t have any friends now. She said she had no time for that sort of thing, but she had told him a bit about how she used to go to parties and meet up with friends with his dad – back when his dad was still alive. She seemed to be sad when she talked about those times – like it hurt her to remember.

“My mum is at work, but I know she’d love to see you,” Ash said.

“Maybe some other time, Ashley. I’m actually here about my son.” She thrust the crumpled-up leaflet towards him. "You gave him this yesterday. I wanted to thank you very much for your offer but to tell you that we won't be accepting."

Ash looked like he didn't understand. He stared down at the leaflet as if he didn't know where it had come from.

"But ... it's just some free sessions, Mrs Marie. Your son is very good. I—"

"We don't need your charity," she snapped. "Thank you all the same, but I don't want any handouts. It's a pity that I can't afford the cost of these expensive football schools, but I won't have some lad coming along and offering my son false hope."

Ash shook his head. "I don't understand."

"What happens when the free sessions stop, eh?" she went on. "What will Lewis do then? You will have given him the taste and he'll want to continue. I won't be able to afford to keep it up."

She took Lewis's hand in hers and started to move him away. "I'm sorry, Ashley. It's very kind of you to offer, but we can't accept."

And she carefully led Lewis away.

Chapter 9

The next day passed slowly. Lewis couldn't bear to go outside and practise, and when Jermaine messaged him and asked if he wanted to meet up, he politely refused – making out he didn't feel well. Instead, he spent most of the day watching YouTube videos on his phone and old match replays. He watched them with the sound down, so as not to upset his mum.

His mind drifted. It had been foolish of him to even think that he could be like one of these players. His life was so different. Why had he been stupid enough to think things could be any other way?

Later in the afternoon, his mum sat beside him. She took his hand.

"I know you feel sad," she said. "But remember what happened to your dad? Football did him no good in the end. He might still be here if it wasn't for that blessed game. Maybe it's a good thing, eh?"

"But I'm not Dad," Lewis whispered.

His mum squeezed his hand. "I know. But it's not only that. Everything is different now he's gone. I could never afford to pay for the clubs, boots and the kit, or to take you to the games …" She shook her head. "I'm sorry."

But Lewis couldn't look at her. Her sorry sounded flat and wrong. He understood that she was worried about money, but she couldn't keep blaming the game for what happened to his dad. He thought of the photo of his dad that was now hidden under his pillow. Of him running down the pitch. The smile on his face was wide and his eyes were blazing with energy.

How could something be so bad if it made someone look so happy?

*

Later that evening, there was a knock on the door. Trevor barked in surprise. Hardly anyone visited them at this time. When his mum opened the door, Lewis heard her voice rise.

"Ashley! I wasn't expecting you."

"Can I come in, Mrs Marie?"

Lewis quickly sat up on the sofa, paused his phone and smoothed down his hair. He knew he must look a right state. He'd been lazing around most of the day.

Ash strode in. He looked down at Lewis's phone, at the match Lewis had been watching, and grinned. "Hey, Chelsea–Arsenal, eh? That was a good one, right?"

Lewis nodded, feeling shy. "It was really tight."

Ash shrugged. "I'm a Chelsea fan, so I'm glad they got that late goal. Who do you support again?"

Lewis's mum walked in behind. "He's Crystal Palace, like his dad."

Ash nodded. "Ah, yes. Of course."

Ash stood there for a moment or two and then turned to face Lewis's mum again. "Mrs Marie, I'm sorry. I couldn't let this go. I really want Lewis to train with us. I hate to see his talent go to waste."

Lewis saw his mum's cheeks turn pink. "But I thought I explained—"

"I know, and I totally understand that. So I'm coming to you with a different offer." Ash smiled. "Lewis can earn his place. He can help me set up for practice and pack away after. He can clean boots, help me with some admin. He'd actually be doing me a big favour because I do need the help."

Lewis felt his heart leap. "I could do that, Mum."

"It would be good work experience for him. It'll keep him busy," Ash added.

"I don't know." Mum frowned. "What about school? Your school still expects you to keep up with your reading in the holidays and didn't they set you some work to do?"

"I don't have much, Mum, and I'll keep reading. I promise," Lewis said.

"It'll keep him busy," Ash said. "And out of trouble."

Lewis's mum sighed. "Well, I suppose it does sound like a good solution." She paused. "But just for the summer, OK? I don't want it affecting school."

Ash nodded. "Sounds good."

She faced Lewis. "And remember, Lewis. This is just a hobby. Something to do for fun. Don't get carried away, OK?"

Lewis grinned. "I promise."

But it would be a difficult promise to keep.

Chapter 10

The following Monday, Lewis arrived early at the Deansgate ground where Ace Academy was based during the holidays. Jermaine had said he could have a lift in his dad's car, but Lewis wanted to get there early. He knew he would have to do a few jobs first to "earn his place".

It was quite a long walk to the other side of town, but he didn't mind. His mum had packed him a small lunch and given him a kiss as he left. "Enjoy it," she'd said with an awkward smile.

Lewis was wearing Jermaine's old football boots, which were a little big, his own PE shorts and a plain white T-shirt. Ash met him at the door. "You can help me set up the equipment," he said. "And sort out the bibs for our match later."

Lewis nodded – that sounded easy enough.

"Don't worry. The lads are friendly here and you know a few of them, don't you?" Ash said.

"Yes. Jermaine and Harry."

Ash laughed. "There you go! You're going to fit in fine!"

Half an hour later, the rest of the boys arrived. Most of them were wearing the strips of their favourite teams and had flash new boots and bags. Lewis knew he looked different, so he sat down quietly next to Jermaine, trying not to stand out.

Jermaine smiled at him and tried to help him make friends with some of the other boys, but Lewis couldn't focus. He felt so nervous.

As he sat and waited, the other boys were talking loudly and laughing. He felt like a ghost in the room. In fact, he'd never felt so out of place before.

When they were all outside, Lewis stood at the back while they started to warm up. Ash was up front, giving instructions with another coach called Ben. They were both loud and bossy, but in a good way.

The boys were told to jog on the spot, to do star jumps, lunges and burpees. Lewis found he could keep up easily. These were things he practised when he was on his own, like he'd seen professionals do on YouTube.

A boy nudged him. He was short and stocky with long dark hair pulled into a ponytail and had a mean-looking snub nose and scowly mouth.

"What's with the boots?" he said, pointing. "They look battered."

"Ah, leave him, Jamie," one of the other boys said.

Lewis felt his cheeks glow red. He knew Jermaine's boots were old and a bit tatty, but it had been good of him to give them to Lewis.

The boy, Jamie, nudged him again. "You have no kit. You look like a tramp."

Lewis glared at him and then quickly moved away. He didn't want to say anything back. He knew he might get angry and lose his temper.

Ash was already shouting a new set of instructions. He was asking the boys to line up at the edge of the field. They were going to do a set of sprints. As they moved into a line, Lewis saw he was standing next to Jamie. Typical. He sucked in a deep breath and turned his face away from him.

"I'm going to thrash you, tramp-boy," Jamie hissed.

Ash blew the whistle and the boys ran.

Lewis could feel his arms and legs burning with energy as he drove himself forward. He

knew he was fast. He usually won the short distance races at school. As they reached the other side, Lewis pressed harder, pushing his chest forward. He cleared the line first – at least two metres ahead of the others.

“Well done, Lewis!” Ash shouted. “You’ve definitely got some speed on you.”

Lewis turned around, grinning. Then he saw Jamie’s face. It was grim and cold.

"You may be good at running," Jamie said. "But let's see how good you are in the game."

Lewis knew it was a threat, but suddenly he wasn't scared. He just needed a chance to show Jamie how good he was.

Chapter 11

The main game was at the end of the session, after lunch. The boys were split into teams and played against each other. Lewis wasn't in the same team as Jermaine or even Jamie, but he was pleased.

He'd been watching Jamie for most of the day and, although the boy was the loudest in the group, he wasn't the most skilful. Lewis was also glad to be placed with boys like Harry, Oscar, Fletcher, Joe and Liam. They could all move the ball well and they seemed to be good team players.

Harry turned to Lewis, grinning. "Where do you want to play?"

Lewis felt a little shy even with his friend. He was still the new boy after all. "Left wing, if that's OK?"

Harry nodded. "Cool. You've always been lucky to be able to choose. I wish I could play with both feet like you can."

"Really?" Oscar said, looking impressed. "I wish I could."

"Honestly, you should see him," Harry replied. "He doesn't even have to try – he can play left- or right-footed. Jermaine and me have always been jealous."

Lewis grinned. Harry and Jermaine were always telling him how cool it was that he could play with both feet. Lewis never used to think it was such a big deal. According to his mum, his dad had been the same. It was just another thing he'd inherited from him.

*

The match was an exciting one.

To begin with, Lewis saw little of the ball and didn't feel confident about shouting for it. But towards the end of the first half, the opposition lost possession near Lewis and he was able to collect the ball by the line and make a run towards goal. There was no option to pass, so instead Lewis used his quick feet to first dribble round one defender and then do a quick turn to unbalance another, Jamie.

The goal was in sight. Lewis saw the keeper come off his line. Without losing a second, Lewis lofted the ball up, high and clear over the keeper's head.

Would it make it?

He could hardly believe it himself as he watched the ball sail into the back of the net. His team-mates crowded round him. Harry slapped him on the back.

"What a goal, Lewis!"

The rest of the game passed in a flash. Lewis felt like he was on fire as he made one and then more darting runs down the wing. He felt confident to call out now and shouted for the ball each time he was in space. By the time Ash blew the whistle, Lewis had set up two goals and scored one other. His team had won 4–1.

Jamie came up behind him after the match, frowning. "You were lucky that time, tramp," he muttered. "Next time you won't be."

Lewis stared back him, stunned. He wasn't sure what to say, but Jamie had already moved off. It didn't matter anyway – the rest of his team were all over Lewis, praising him for his skills. They didn't notice Jamie.

Lewis walked back in with the other boys, no longer feeling left out. As he got changed, he moved to be next to Harry. Luckily Jamie was on the other side of the room.

The others chatted to Lewis. Suddenly it no longer mattered that he had the wrong kit or old tatty boots. He had shown that he belonged, that he deserved a place.

As Lewis was getting ready to leave, Ash came and sat down next to him. He had the biggest smile on his face and he turned so as to talk to Lewis one on one.

"You OK, mate? Did you enjoy today?" he asked.

Lewis nodded. "It's been great."

"You did really well. Ben commented on how fast you are and how good you were at the dribbling exercise." Then Ashley went on, "But it was in the game where you really stood out.

It was like you came alive. That first goal was pretty impressive, and your runs cut through the defence so easily." He nodded. "You're really good, you know?"

"Thanks," Lewis said shyly. "I just wanted to try my best, that's all."

"You definitely did that." Ash waited a moment. "There's a tournament coming up at the end of the month. I wasn't going to say anything about it as you're so new here, but I think you should play. Some important people will be there."

"Really? You think?"

"I think you'd be an asset to the team," Ash said. "And you can invite your mum along. She can see how good you really are."

Lewis didn't say anything. He really wasn't sure his mum would want to come.

"You can ask anyway," Ash suggested. "You never know."

"Yeah, sure," Lewis replied.

"Good," Ash said, grinning. He went to move away and then quickly turned back. "I know about your dad, you know. He used to play at Deansgate like me. I heard he was an amazing player."

Lewis couldn't meet his eyes. "He was."

"It looks like you might take after him." Ash paused. "He'd be proud of you."

"Thank you."

"Oh, and take no notice of Jamie – he's all mouth that one. He's OK when you get to know him. I think he's just a bit jealous of your skills. It's like you're a threat to him."

"Me? A threat?" Lewis was puzzled. How could he be a threat to anyone?

"Believe me, kid. You stand out," Ash said. "And in the very best way."

Chapter 12

The next few weeks flew by. Lewis was enjoying every second of his time at Ace Academy. His mum didn't ask him much about the days, but Lewis didn't mind. He was too happy to let it worry him.

Alongside Jermaine and Harry, Cole and Charlie were becoming good friends and he found that most of the time he could ignore Jamie's evil looks and mutters. Jamie was a decent footballer, strong and confident, but he lacked the skills and speed that Lewis had. Lewis tried not to let Jamie's words hurt him.

Even so, in practice sessions, Jamie was hard with tackles, as if he was trying to catch Lewis out. Luckily Lewis was quick and shook them off. He didn't lose his temper or react to Jamie. His mum had told him that his dad was always calm on the pitch. He never lost his temper. Lewis wanted to be the same.

But towards the end of the third week, Jamie was in a really bad mood. They were playing another practice match and Lewis was once again on the opposing side to Jamie.

Everything started fine. Jamie was playing at left back, so was nowhere near him. Lewis was making some good runs on the left wing and crossed one ball in to his striker, Cole, who powered the ball into the net. The match restarted and Lewis saw that Jamie had switched to right back and was now marking him.

Lewis quickly got another chance to make a run down the wing. He looked up and saw that

Jamie was bearing down on him. He tried to turn him, to move the ball away from him, but Jamie was determined. He could see it in his face.

Lewis knew something was wrong as soon as he saw Jamie's leg come up. He felt a terrible pain as Jamie tripped him up, making Lewis crash to the ground.

The other boys surrounded them. They immediately began shouting at Jamie.

"That was out of order. You went in high!"

"You took him out on purpose."

"You've hurt him bad, Jamie!"

Lewis sat up, still holding his throbbing leg. Ash ran over to them and Jamie stared down at Lewis where he lay on the pitch.

"I'm sorry, Lewis," Jamie muttered, his face pale and scared. "I just lost it."

Lewis couldn't talk. His thigh was red and sore and it hurt to move. He felt sick.

Was this it? Was his football playing over already?

Had his mum been right all along?

Chapter 13

Back in the hall, Lewis sat with his leg stretched out in front of him and an ice pack clamped to his skin. Ash was next to him. His face was grim.

"I'm so sorry, Lewis. Jamie will be dealt with," Ash said firmly. "He won't be playing in the tournament now, that's for sure. I won't let players with that kind of attitude take part."

Lewis shrugged. He didn't feel angry with Jamie. He just felt let down and worried. He didn't want an injury to affect his game.

Ash leaned forward and looked at the bruise on Lewis's leg. "It looks bad. But if you rest it over the next few days, keep ice on it and keep it raised – I think it will be fine." He went on, "You'll have to miss the next few sessions though."

"Can I still watch?" Lewis asked. "I have my jobs to do after all."

Ash smiled. "You don't have to worry about those jobs, mate. Not at the moment. But sure, come and watch if you like. We'd love that."

"And what about the tournament?"

Lewis was counting the days down in his head. The first tournament was next weekend. Would he recover in time? Would he get enough practice in?

"If your leg is better by next Friday, you can play," Ash said. "But don't put pressure on yourself. There will be other games."

Lewis nodded. He knew this of course. But right now this was the only game that mattered.

*

Back at home, Mum fussed over his leg. Trevor even gave it a quick lick, like he knew something was wrong.

"Look at the size of the bruise," she said, stroking his skin. "You're lucky your leg's not broken."

"It's fine, Mum. It doesn't even hurt as bad now."

"It looks very sore to me." She stepped back, crossing her arms. "This is what I was worried about – you hurting yourself. After what happened to your dad—"

"This isn't like what happened to my dad."

She sniffed. “Even so, I don’t like seeing you hurt like this. Does this mean you will be stopping now?”

Lewis frowned. "No, Mum. I'm still going to go to the sessions and watch the boys. I'm still hoping I can make the tournament next Saturday."

"Tournament?" His mum looked confused. "Where's that?"

"At Deansgate football ground. Ash says there will be loads of teams there and some important people too. Scouts. He really wants me to play."

She frowned. "I see."

"Mum, can you come? I'd really like you to be there."

His mum looked away. "Next Saturday you say? I think I'm busy, Lewis. I agreed to do some more cleaning shifts."

"But it's the afternoon, Mum. You never work then."

"I'm sorry, Lewis. I'm busy," she said firmly. She stared back at him. Her eyes were sad now. "Go if you want to. I hope you do well, I really do, but I can't be there. I'm sorry."

And then she quickly left the room.

Chapter 14

Lewis could hardly believe the day of the tournament was here. He was fizzing with nerves. As he got out of bed, he inspected his leg. The bruise had turned a nasty green-grey colour now, but his thigh no longer hurt to move.

"I think I'm going to be OK, Trevor," he said.

Trevor licked his hand. Lewis took that to mean that he agreed. He ruffled Trev's ears.

"Wish me luck," he whispered. "I think I'll really need it today."

The fizzy feeling in his stomach didn't go as he made his way to the ground with Jermaine. Jermaine's dad was giving them a lift in the car.

"It's going to be amazing," Jermaine said to him. "We get to play the best teams around. You're going to love it."

Lewis nodded. He knew he would enjoy it, but he couldn't help thinking about his mum saying goodbye to him in the kitchen before she left for work earlier. She had seemed so tired and sad. He only wished she could be with him today too.

"You're both going to be great," Jermaine's dad said proudly.

"Thanks," Lewis replied softly.

Not only was his mum missing, but he was missing his dad too. Instead of the fizzy feeling, he now just felt very sad.

*

Jermaine and Lewis found the team warming up at the side of the ground. Lewis saw that Jamie was in his tracksuit, standing off to one side.

"Jamie's just watching today," Jermaine said. "It's his punishment."

Lewis frowned. He actually felt a bit bad for Jamie. He knew what Jamie had done was out of order, but he knew how bad he must be feeling to miss this tournament. Before he could stop himself, he walked over to him.

"Hey, Jamie."

Jamie looked up and scowled. "I guess you're happy now."

"Not at all," Lewis said. "I never wanted you to miss the game."

Jamie shrugged. "Someone had to. We have a big squad." He waited a moment. "And to be fair, you played out of your skin at training."

Lewis smiled. "Cheers."

"I'm really sorry I went in hard. I shouldn't have done that. Ash said I was lucky – I could've done real damage."

"Yeah, I guess it's lucky I'm so light. I just bounced." Lewis paused. "But maybe don't do it again."

Jamie nodded. "Good luck today, yeah? Help us win this."

"I'll try."

Chapter 15

The tournament flew past quickly. The day was made up of lots of short matches, ending up with a big final.

Lewis played in three of the four qualifying games and his team won them all. Even better, Lewis had set up six of their ten goals and scored three of them. He was feeling good.

And when they got to the final, they were up against Felton Academy, one of the best teams in the south.

Lewis was on the left wing for the final game – his favourite position. He jiggled up and down on the spot, waiting for the game to start. Ash had spoken to them all at the beginning. He'd told them to try their best and work together as a team.

Lewis scanned the crowd, but he couldn't see anyone he knew.

The whistle blew.

The game passed in a blur. Lewis made lots of runs on the ball. At first his team-mates weren't passing the ball to him. All of the action was on the right side and a defensive error soon meant that Lewis's team were 0–1 down.

But minutes later their keeper passed to Lewis and, looking up, he couldn't see any outfield players to pass to. So instead he took the ball on. He dribbled past two defenders and then neatly passed the ball into the box for Jermaine to place into the back of the net: 1–1.

And then, just before the final whistle, Lewis spotted the keeper off his line. He picked up the ball at the edge of the box and slotted a shot into the top right-hand corner.

2–1.

Lewis was sure he could hear Ash's cheers from where he stood. His team-mates surrounded him, sweeping him up in hugs and thumping him on the back.

Lewis looked up, his eyes blinking back the tears.

He could hardly believe what had just happened.

And then he saw her, standing in the crowd, watching. Her smile the brightest of them all. Trevor was sitting proudly beside her. She had come.

His mum.

Chapter 16

Later, the boys were all together with their medals in their hands. Harry was holding the trophy aloft. Ash was going round to each of them in turn, giving praise. Then a tall man with a clipboard walked up and he and Ash went off together.

Lewis's mum came over and pulled Lewis towards her. "I'm sorry," she said. "I was being so selfish before."

"I'm just glad you came," Lewis replied.

"I was being silly and stubborn. I wasn't sure I could come back here, to the Deansgate ground," she said softly. "But I can't keep living in the past. What happened to your dad won't happen to you. He had a heart condition. He was unlucky. It wasn't football that killed him."

"I know," Lewis said. "You just didn't like to talk about it."

She patted his arm. "It was easier to blame football than something I couldn't understand, like simple bad luck." She sighed. "I forgot how happy football made him. Until I saw you play, and then I remembered. You look just like him, you know."

Lewis felt warm and happy. "Do I?"

"You really do."

They heard someone cough and turned to see Ash standing there next to the tall man with the clipboard. They were both smiling. Ash turned to Lewis.

"Lewis, I wanted to introduce you to Ross Green. He's the head scout at Deansgate. He saw you play today and was really impressed."

"Scout?" his mum repeated, shocked.

Ross grinned. "That's right. I'd like to sign Lewis up for a trial at our academy. I think he has lots of potential and he's just what we're looking for."

"Seriously?" Lewis said, hardly able to believe it. "You want me?"

Ash laughed out loud. "You need to start believing, Lewis. Your journey is just starting."

*

Back home, Lewis sat with his dad's photo again. He'd pulled it out from under his pillow and was holding it in full view. This time his mum and Trevor were next to him. They were wrapped together in a tight warm ball. Trevor was snoring softly.

"I love this photo," Lewis said. "It's my very favourite."

"Mine too," his mum said softly. She stroked his hair. "I mustn't hide it any more. Your dad would hate that. I'll put it out with the others."

Lewis smiled.

"Your dad would be so proud of you," she said.

"I wish he could see me though."

"I think he can, you know," she replied. "He lives on inside of you. He is part of you. Always."

Lewis snuggled up closer to his mum. He liked that thought. It made him feel good.

"Can you tell me more about him, Mum?" he whispered. "I want to know more. I want to know everything."

"Of course," she replied. "Where do I begin?"

And as the night slowly settled on their tower block, his mum finally began to talk.